CommBank MATILDAS

FOOTBALL AUSTRALIA PRESENTS

SOCCEROOS

FOOTBALL FEVER

FOOTBALL FEVER

HALF-TIME HEROES

KRISTIN DARELL

ILLUSTRATIONS BY LESLEY VAMOS

PUFFIN BOOKS

PUFFIN BOOKS

UK | USA | Canada | Ireland | Australia
India | New Zealand | South Africa | China

Penguin Random House Australia

Penguin Random House Australia is part of the Penguin Random House group of companies whose addresses can be found at global.penguinrandomhouse.com.

First published by Puffin Books, an imprint of Penguin Random House Australia Pty Ltd, in 2023

Cover design by Caroline Lee © Penguin Random House Australia Pty Ltd
Illustrations by Lesley Vamos
Internal design and typesetting by Midland Typesetters, Australia

Printed and bound in Australia by Griffin Press, an accredited
ISO AS/NZS 14001 Environmental Management Systems printer

NATIONAL LIBRARY OF AUSTRALIA
A catalogue record for this book is available from the National Library of Australia

ISBN 978 1 76 104807 4

penguin.com.au

We at Penguin Random House Australia acknowledge that Aboriginal and Torres Strait Islander peoples are the Traditional Custodians and the first storytellers of the lands on which we live and work. We honour Aboriginal and Torres Strait Islander peoples' continuous connection to Country, waters, skies and communities. We celebrate Aboriginal and Torres Strait Islander stories, traditions and living cultures; and we pay our respects to Elders past and present.

CHAPTER 1

'Ugh, it's hopeless!'

Sasha shut her laptop and let out a dramatic groan as she flopped back on the cushions littering her lounge-room floor.

'Come on, Sasha,' Finn said, smiling at his best friend. 'You're going to nail it.'

She sat up and looked at him, eyes narrowed. 'Really?'

Finn kept smiling. 'Really!' He opened the laptop. 'Your project is going to be awesome. Everything you do always is.' Sasha was super good on the computer. Almost as good as she was at football. The problem was the topic her teacher had set: *The four most important people or things in your life*. She'd interviewed Finn as her best friend, and she planned to do some stuff about football and her team, the Merridale Fever. But she was freaking out about how to include her dads.

Sasha stood up and walked to a large glass tank sitting on a bench. She opened the door of the enclosure and scooped up her pygmy bearded dragon. Sasha took a deep breath in and out.

'What if people, you know, say stuff?' she said quietly, looking at the dragon as she stroked its back.

'What if they do?' Finn asked. 'You have an insanely cool life. Two dads who are on TV, a dragon and the awesome-est best friend in the world.'

'You know awesome-est isn't a word, right?' Sasha said, one corner of her mouth turned up as she looked at him.

Finn slapped his forehead. '*That's* the bit you heard?'

Sasha grinned. 'You're right,' she said. 'Here, hold Grogu.' She placed the dragon in Finn's palm, then plonked down in front of the computer. Two seconds later, she jumped back up. 'Nuts. Training's in ten minutes.' Sasha shut the laptop. 'Can you put Grogu away? I'll ask Paps to walk us to the oval.'

'Sure,' Finn said. He wished he had Sasha's energy. They went to different schools but had been best friends since starting football together at Merridale FC in the U8s. At their first training session,

Sasha had given him a hair band – she'd thought it was cool that his hair was longer than hers – and three years later, they were still in the same team. The Merridale Fever U11s were having their best season ever. Coach was teaching them more complicated gameplays, they were focusing on specific positions and they'd had three wins from three games.

Finn loved going to Sasha's house before Monday training. Hanging out with his football family helped take his mind off his mum being sick again. She wasn't up to doing much while she had chemotherapy. His dad had promised it was fine, but Finn still felt guilty about leaving his little brother, Xavier, at home. It helped that his mum was a huge football fan, so he knew she wanted him to do what he loved. Thinking about his mum made

Finn's chest hurt. But it gave him extra motivation to keep trying hard.

'Let's go, Finn,' Sasha called.

'Coming,' he said. Finn gently put Grogu back in his tank and locked it before heading for the front of the house. 'Hi Mr Parry.'

'Hey Finn,' he said. 'How's your mum going with the chemo?'

Finn swallowed. 'She's okay.'

Mr Parry gave him a gentle smile. 'Well, remember, you and Xavier are welcome here any time.'

Finn nodded. 'Thanks.'

It was only three blocks to the oval. As they crossed the car park, Finn saw a bunch of kids dressed in their Merridale yellow and green training jerseys, kicking balls. He waved to Old Noel cleaning the barbecue outside the clubhouse. Noel waved back. Everyone loved Noel.

'Sasha, I just messaged you the link to the video,' Mr Parry said. 'I've already sent Coach the form.'

Finn heard Sasha's phone ping.

'I've got to head off. You guys okay?' Mr Parry asked.

'You bet,' Sasha said, giving him a quick hug. 'See you after.'

'What video?' Finn asked as Mr Parry headed back up the street.

Sasha shuffled her feet, eyes down. 'I was going to wait and surprise you with everyone else, but . . .' She held up the message. Finn peered at the small screen. It said: *Half-time Heroes Competition Now Open!*

‘When did you find out?’ Finn said. ‘What do we have to do?’ He crossed his arms. ‘And why didn’t you tell me?’

Sasha looked sheepish. ‘Sorry, but I think it’ll be fun for us all to look at it together.’

‘Come on, Sasha. You can tell –’

‘Nope.’ She turned her phone screen off. ‘But trust me, you’re going to love it.’

Sasha’s mouth was smiling, but her eyes weren’t. It was what Finn called a worry smile. His dad used it when talking about his mum being sick. Finn knew Sasha wasn’t telling him something, but he couldn’t imagine what, or why. She’d never kept a secret from him before. He pushed the feeling away. He’d find out soon enough.

CHAPTER 2

Sasha didn't like keeping a secret from Finn. He looked so disappointed. Crouching down to put her phone in her bag gave her an excuse to avoid his eye. She felt awful. She'd already watched the video, but she couldn't tell him her Half-time Heroes idea yet. Her gut told her he wasn't going to love it, and her dads always told her to trust her gut. They'd also taught her that when she was worried, she should breathe.

Deep breath in. Hold. Slowly breathe out.

Breathing helped keep her calm. She knew she shouldn't worry so much, but she couldn't help it.

'Enough talking, more kicking!'

Sasha looked up at the sound of Kyra's voice. She was walking past with the Fever's other striker, Sam. They were carrying two mini goals. Kyra's dog, Diego, was trotting at their side, his tongue flapping around.

'*You* can talk!' Sasha fired back, avoiding Finn's eyes.

Kyra and Sam laughed as they headed onto the pitch. Sasha and Finn jogged after them.

Everyone liked Kyra – she was the Fever's chatterbox – and everyone loved Diego. Named after football superstar Diego Maradona, the golden retriever was their team mascot and chief ball chaser. Kyra had started with Merridale in the U6s. Sam, on the other hand, had recently moved to Australia from England. He'd had a bit of a rough start – playing football on a mixed team wasn't what he was used to, and Kyra hadn't been able to understand at first. But they'd figured it out and now, three games into the season, Sam and Kyra were an unstoppable goal-scoring duo.

Sasha put her bag down, then sat on a bench to tighten her laces. Finn had twisted his long hair into a band and scooped up a ball. He bounced it off his knee and caught it. She smiled at the surprised look on his face. But it also gave her hope. While she found tricks fun and easy, Finn usually struggled, which was why she was so worried about her Half-time Heroes idea.

Sasha took another breath as Diego burrowed his head under her hand for a pat.

Stroking the dog's soft white fur, Sasha watched her teammates muck around. They were all there now. Sam was kicking in a circle with Kyra, Harper, Hani and the twins, Kat and Luka. Charlie and Ava were practising juggling while Meili and Crabbie chatted. Given the way Crabbie was shuffling sideways and waving his hands around, Sasha knew he was talking about Andrew Redmayne's penalty save to get the Socceroos into the 2022 World Cup. It was their red-haired goalkeeper's favourite topic.

Her breathing felt a little easier now. This was her team. The Merridale Fever. Playing at half-time in a Socceroos match at Accor Stadium in front of a huge crowd would be a dream come true for them all. They just had to make one short video. How hard could it be?

Coach called the team over. Justine Williams – also Kyra's mum – had been a star defender in the Young Matildas, but luckily for them, she'd decided to focus on coaching. Whether Coach was working with the Fever as a group, or helping Sasha one-on-one, she always made Sasha believe that her dream of playing for the CommBank Matildas was possible.

'Another fantastic game last weekend,' Coach said. 'I'm so proud of how well you're playing as a team. Let's warm up.'

Week four and the Fever knew the drill. They always started with a jog – forwards then backwards, between two cones. Today that was followed by criss-crosses, knee-ups and walking lunges. Then a lap kicking their heels up behind them.

'While you stretch, I'll explain what's happening today,' Coach said. 'We're going to focus on one activity – a midfield game drill. Then I've left some time at the end for Sasha to share some exciting news with you all.'

Sasha kept her eyes down as she stretched her calves, but she could sense her teammates glancing her way.

'We're playing piggy in the middle,' Coach continued. Sasha let out a breath as the focus shifted away from her. 'You'll be in three teams,' Coach said. 'One team will start in this goal third. They have to get the ball to the team waiting near the other goal. But,' Coach smiled, 'the third team will be in the middle, trying to steal the ball. If they do, or when a team scores, we rotate.' Coach looked around the group. 'Got it?'

'Yes, Coach!' they all called out.

Sasha was with Harper and Crabbie. They had the ball first, but they had to get past Sam, Kat and Ava. Coach blew the whistle. Sasha felt a rush of adrenalin. Harper dribbled the ball up the centre. Sam raced forward to tackle her.

'Harper,' Sasha called out. Harper slid the ball her way as she ran along the sideline. Kat was on her, fast.

Stay low. Arms out. Protect the ball.

Crabbie ran forward. Sasha narrowed her eyes. She faked right, then cut left, making enough space to pass. She kicked hard. Crabbie stopped the ball. Sasha darted around Kat, calling out. Crabbie flicked the ball back and she pushed it past Ava to where Finn was waiting in the goal third. He turned and shot. He scored. She grinned. They made a great team.

'Nice play, Sasha,' Kat said as she jogged past to reset.

This time Sasha's team was in the middle.

Defending was harder, but midfield was where she loved to play, so she gave it everything she had. They rotated through all three thirds, three times. Sasha was puffing when Coach finally blew the whistle, ending the drill.

'Great work, everyone. Please bring the cones and balls back in,' Coach said. 'It's time for Sasha's news.'

Sasha looked at her watch. She'd been having so much fun, she hadn't realised training was almost over. Her smile faded as she gathered balls with Diego's help, then grabbed her phone out of her bag.

'I have to pop to the clubhouse,' Coach said. She winked at Sasha. 'Over to you.'

Sasha felt eleven sets of eyes focus on her. She *had* been bursting to tell her teammates. But now . . .

CHAPTER 3

Finn could see Sasha gripping her phone as she watched Coach walk away. He didn't get it. They were her teammates. He was her best friend.

What's she so worried about?

He would have smiled to reassure her, but she wouldn't look his way. Something definitely wasn't right.

Sasha took a deep breath. 'So, you've probably guessed it's about Half-time

Heroes,' she said. 'Well, um, the competition's officially open.'

'Yes!' Crabbie said, pumping his fist. 'What do we have to do?'

Sasha unlocked her phone. 'Remember I told you it would be a team challenge?' she said. 'This video explains it.'

They all crowded around. Sasha clicked play.

Two familiar faces appeared on the screen: CommBank Matildas defender Courtney Nevin and Socceroos forward Marco Tilio.

'Hey everyone,' Marco said with a wave and a smile. 'The Half-time Heroes competition is back.'

'That's right,' Courtney added. 'And here's your challenge, should you choose to accept it. We want you to record a video that shows us what makes *your* MiniRoos team special.'

'You can do anything you like,' Marco said. 'You can talk, you can show us your skills. It's entirely up to you.'

'The two winning clubs will play at half-time during the Socceroos friendly against the USA at Accor Stadium next month,' Courtney continued.

'That means we need your entries next week,' Marco said. 'So, you don't have long.'

'Well, what are you waiting for?' Courtney asked.

'See you on the pitch!' Courtney and Marco finished together, then the Football Australia logo appeared.

Sasha switched off her phone.

'Next week!' Meili exclaimed, eyes wide.

'What should we do?' Harper asked.

Finn saw Sasha glance his way.

'I think we should do a video showing off tricks,' she said. 'Remember the MiniRoos Trick Star competition?' Sasha was talking quickly now. 'Tricks will look awesome in a video.'

Finn couldn't believe what he was hearing.

Tricks. Seriously?!

Sasha knew he couldn't do tricks. She also knew how much being a Half-time Hero meant to him and his whole family.

He looked at his teammates. Kyra and Sam were nodding. Meili and Charlie seemed happy too. His chest felt tight.

'Tricks with us wearing Merridale's yellow and green, Australia's colours,' Kyra said. 'This is going to be so good! Maybe we can get a club shirt for Diego too.'

'Woof!'

Kyra gave him a scratch on the head.

'But what if we can't do tricks?' Finn asked quietly.

'Exactly,' Kat said, stepping up beside him. 'Tricks aren't for everyone.'

'And it's not like we have much time to learn them either,' Crabbie added.

Finn saw Sasha fidgeting. She did that when she was worried. 'But we need to stand out, and tricks always look cool.'

'I'm not saying tricks *aren't* cool,' Finn said. 'It's just not about us as a *team*,' he added, looking straight at Sasha.

'*You* suggest something, then,' Sasha said. Her arms were crossed, and her cheeks were red.

Finn kicked his football boot into the grass. He'd never seen Sasha like this. It was like she'd picked the one thing she knew he didn't feel confident doing. And she wanted to make a video about it! She was supposed to be his best friend. This was about *all* the Merridale Fever, wasn't it? Everyone had a say.

'I don't know,' Finn said. He couldn't think with everyone looking at him.

There was some murmuring, but no-one else spoke. The silence started to get loud, until Coach came back from the clubhouse.

'I'd expected a bit more excitement from you all,' Coach said to the team. 'The chance to play at a Socceroos game!'

'We were just talking about what to put in the video,' Sasha said quietly.

'Ah,' Coach said. Finn wasn't the only one who struggled to make eye contact as she looked around the team. He saw Coach raise her eyebrows. 'It's not an easy decision, and it'll involve some compromise. But now it's home time, so why don't you think about it and talk more at training on Thursday? I can give you some time to try things out.'

Finn kicked a stray ball back to the pile as he watched his teammates grab their things and drift off. They were all chatting happily. Even Kat and Crabbie seemed excited again. Was he the only one still feeling weird? Finn sighed. Sasha was standing next to his bag, talking to Kyra and Meili, and he couldn't avoid going over any longer.

'. . . and I'm sure we can find something,' Kyra was saying. 'Right, Finn?'

'Um, yeah, sure,' he stuttered.

'I mean, we have to, right?' Kyra continued. 'We *have* to be Half-time Heroes. Mum told me sometimes Matildas players even help. Can you imagine?'

Finn smiled. It was hard not to get caught up in Kyra's excitement. He glanced at Sasha, but she still wouldn't meet his eye. His smile faded.

Sasha looked towards the car park. 'Gotta go,' she said. 'Dad and Paps are here.'

'Hey, how about we meet at the Fever Creek House tomorrow after school,' Meili suggested. 'I can message everyone, and we can try to come up with more video ideas.'

'I've got a school project to get done, but I'll check with my dads,' Sasha said. 'An hour should be okay.'

'I'm in,' Kyra said. 'Mum will be here anyway.'

'Great.' Meili smiled. 'Finn?'

He shook his head. 'Sorry, I've got to help look after Xavier while Dad takes Mum to do some stuff.'

‘No worries,’ Meili said. ‘Keep thinking, though!’

‘Sure,’ Finn said. He bent down to pick up his bag. When he looked up, Sasha had gone. He watched her walk towards the car park. She hadn’t even said goodbye. Finn frowned. First the trick thing, now she was ignoring him.

What have I done wrong?

CHAPTER 4

Sasha sipped orange juice as she listened to Kyra, Meili, Kat, Luka and Sam talk inside the Fever Creek House. They'd shifted the catch-up to Wednesday, but still only half the team had made it. Sasha had hoped the change would make it possible for Finn to come. Apart from a short message on the group chat, she hadn't heard from him or seen him since he'd ignored her at the end of Monday training. Nada, nothing. They normally messaged every day.

Sasha pressed her lips together. She wasn't going to feel bad. She hadn't done anything wrong.

Sasha took another sip of juice and looked around. The Fever Creek House always made her feel better. Kyra and Meili had found the small, abandoned building across the creek behind Merridale Oval when they were in the U8s. The club had checked it out and given them permission to do it up, and it had been the Fever's special meeting place ever since.

Sasha looked at the posters of the CommBank Matildas and Socceroos stuck on the walls. She sighed. She loved football so much, and she loved her team. She knew they could be Half-time Heroes. They just needed a plan.

'Now, what about our team video?' Sam asked.

Finally!

Sasha let out a breath and gripped the seat to stop her hands shaking. 'I've come up with a list of tricks we could try,' she said quietly.

'But we talked about that –' Kat said.

'I know,' Sasha interrupted. 'That's why I've found tricks that look good but are easy to learn.'

Kat crossed her arms. 'Maybe not easy for everyone,' she muttered.

Sasha's cheeks felt hot.

'What sort of tricks?' Luka asked.

Sasha gave him a grateful smile. 'Well, things like catching the ball on your foot, or a heel juggle. A rainbow flick isn't too hard to learn either.'

'Imagine us all in a line doing rainbow flicks one after the other,' Kyra said. 'That would look awesome.'

'Woof!'

'Diego likes that idea too,' Kyra laughed.

But not everyone was happy.

'I don't,' Kat said, frowning. 'A flick isn't easy for some of us: Finn, Crabbie, Harper and me for a start.' She sighed. 'Finn said it at training: there must be something other than tricks we can do. Being a Half-time Hero means a lot to me too, you know.'

'How about speed dribbling?' Sam asked. 'We've been practising that.'

Sasha shook her head, blinking back tears that had suddenly started to form.

'But *I* can't do that well,' she said. 'And I'm not the only one. Plus, it doesn't look as cool as tricks. Right?'

The creek house fell silent. Diego shuffled over and rested his head on Sasha's lap.

'Coach said she'd give us time at training tomorrow,' Meili said. 'We could try some tricks and see what the others have come up with. Then we can decide.'

Sasha smiled at their tiny, dark-haired goalie.

Kat nodded. 'Okay.'

Kyra's phone buzzed. 'I gotta go. Who's coming?'

Everyone but Sasha stood up. 'I'm going to stay for a bit,' she said. 'Paps won't be long.'

'No worries. See you at training.' Kyra grinned. 'Don't forget your list of tricks.'

Sasha's heart felt heavy, but she managed a smile as Kat, Luka and Sam headed out, followed by Kyra and Diego.

'It'll be okay,' Meili said, pausing at the door and giving Sasha an encouraging smile. 'We're the Fever, aren't we?'

'I suppose,' Sasha said.

Alone in the creek house, Sasha thought about Meili's words. They *were* the Fever, and this video was supposed to show what made them special.

'Argh.' Sasha rested her head in her hands. 'What does that even mean?'

She was having the same problem with her school project, about what was important in her life. She had to include her dads – her family was everything to her, even if they were different from most of her friends. But still . . .

How do you explain that in a Google slide?

Sasha took a deep breath in and out. One thing at a time. First, they had to get this video done. She looked at the poster of the CommBank Matildas. Being on that poster one day was Sasha's dream, and being a Half-time Hero and playing at the

Socceroos match felt like one step closer. All they had to do was make a video, as a team.

We can do this.

As Sasha closed the door of the Fever Creek House, she was determined: she would fight for what she believed was right. She just hoped that she wouldn't lose her best friend in the process.

CHAPTER 5

Thursday. Training day. Normally Finn would be pumped. Today, he wasn't sure he even wanted to go. Sasha hadn't sent him a single message since training on Monday. Not even to rant about her school project.

At least he wouldn't have to show up to training alone – Hani would be with him.

'Earth to Finn,' Hani said. They were passing a football back and forth in Finn's backyard. Finn's little brother, Xavier, was trying to juggle from foot to foot. He'd only just started to learn but was already pretty good.

'Look at me! Look at me!' Xavier said.

Hani and Finn watched as he dropped the ball, lightly flicked it with one foot then hopped as he swapped the ball to the other foot before he flicked the ball up and caught it.

'Yes!' Xavier threw his hands in the air as the boys clapped.

Finn loved his quirky little brother. Xavier was already better at juggling than he was, and he was only eight!

'Xavier, time to do your reading,' Finn's mum called down from the back deck.

Finn looked up. His mum was smiling. She had a bright scarf wrapped around her head. She was having a good day.

'Hi Hani,' she said. 'How are you?'

‘I’m great, thanks,’ Hani said. ‘We’re going to be Half-time Heroes!’

‘*If* we win the competition,’ Finn added.

‘I’m sure you’ll be amazing,’ his mum said. ‘It would be incredible to see you all play at Accor Stadium.’

Finn smiled at his mum, but his chest felt tight. It *would* be incredible. He just hoped she’d be well enough to come if they did win. He also knew none of it mattered if the team couldn’t agree on the video.

What was Sasha thinking? Finn thought. *She knows I’m not good at tricks! She didn’t even ask me about it first.*

He sat on the back steps. Hani plonked down beside him.

‘I’m not sure the video should be about tricks,’ Finn said quietly. ‘I know what Sasha thinks, but . . .’ His voice trailed off.

'Tricks aren't really my thing either,' Hani admitted. 'I know what she's saying about them looking cool, though.'

'Yeah,' Finn said. 'But . . . what if we could make skills look cool?'

Hani turned to face him. 'Like what?'

'Um, a Cruyff turn?' Finn said. 'Or the Ronaldo chop?'

Hani stood up. 'Or a Maradona, or a Rabona. I've been working on both of those.'

'Yeah.' Finn stood up too. At least Hani understood. *Hani* was being a good friend.

'Let's write a list,' Hani said, smiling. 'This is going to be massive.'

Finn felt a flutter of excitement in his stomach. Maybe this was the answer. It would tick Sasha's look-cool box and be something they could *all* do. Finn just had to get everyone to agree.

*

Finn was happy as he walked with Hani to the edge of the Merridale Oval car park. He was sure Sasha would love his idea for the video, and their friendship would go back to normal. There were only a few days left until the deadline, so he had to convince the rest of the team today.

'Hey, check it out,' Hani said. He was pointing towards the clubhouse. Finn had been so caught up in his thoughts he'd missed the cameras and lights.

'Whoa,' Finn said.

'Hey guys.' Charlie jogged up, stopping between Hani and Finn. 'What's going on?'

Hani pointed.

'Is that . . .' Charlie started, squinting.

'It's Awer Mabil,' Finn finished, not quite believing his eyes. The star Socceroos midfielder, his hero, was standing outside the Merridale clubhouse.

'Did you see –' Crabbie said, puffing as he raced up.

'Yes!' Finn, Hani and Charlie answered together with a laugh.

Crabbie's freckles were standing out against his pinker-than-normal face.

'OMG. Did you see who's here?' They heard Sasha's excited voice a second before she burst into the group.

'Yes, Awer Ma–' Charlie started.

'No,' Sasha interrupted. 'I mean, yes. He is. That's cool. But so is Emily van Egmond. *The* Emily van Egmond. CommBank Matildas number 10.'

Finn smiled at his best friend. Her eyes were shining with excitement at seeing her hero. Selected for the national team at fifteen but then injured, Emily had been sixteen when she made her Matildas debut. Sasha often talked about how inspiring it was that Emily had refused to give up. Sasha was stubborn too. She grinned at Finn, their Half-time Heroes disagreement forgotten, for the moment at least.

'What are *they* doing here?' Kat said, pushing her way in between Crabbie and Charlie.

Finn looked around. The whole team was in an excited huddle, Diego running laps around them. Even Coach was there, grinning.

'They're filming some videos for Football Australia,' Coach explained. 'The Socceroos turned a hundred in June 2022. Merridale FC's one of the oldest clubs in Australia. So, they're sharing some of our stories.'

'Will we get to meet them?' Crabbie asked.

Finn could see a few kids being moved away by their coaches.

'Maybe after training,' Coach said. 'If they're finished, *and* you concentrate.'

'Well, let's get going,' Crabbie said, a huge grin stretching across his face.

Coach laughed. 'The gear's in my car.'

They'd never set up so quickly. Even Diego joined in, racing in and out of cones and kids. Finn laughed. This was the Fever he loved.

I hope they like my idea.

Finn glanced at Sasha. She was laughing. He'd missed her over the past week, but being a Half-time Hero was important too. If they couldn't agree, Finn didn't know what he would do.

CHAPTER 6

After warm-up, Coach called the Fever back. Even with her worries about Finn, the video and her school project, Sasha couldn't stop grinning. Emily van Egmond was there, at Merridale FC!

'Now,' Coach said, 'it's Thursday and that means . . .'

'Quiz time!' they called out.

'Correct. Today's football fact is connected to something we've been working on,' Coach explained. 'I'm going to use a drill as an example, but you aren't all going to do it. I know how much the video means to you, so I want to give you plenty of time to work on it.' She grinned and glanced towards the clubhouse. 'Besides, I think there might be a few too many distractions for any *serious* training.'

Everyone laughed.

'Ready, Coach,' Hani said. There were a few groans, but Sasha smiled. Hani's football memory was amazing. He almost always figured out the fact first and won the prize: a voucher for a slushie from Old Noel at the canteen.

'Charlie, Ava and Luka, I'll get you to demonstrate,' Coach said. 'Ava, you stand there.' She pointed to a spot just outside the penalty box. 'Charlie, at the top of the box. Luka, you'll be our goalie.' She turned to face the rest of the team.

'The drill is called Control – Skill – Shoot,' Coach said. 'Ava, I'll pass you the ball. You stop it. That's the control part. Then use a skill to get around Charlie. Last, shoot at goal.'

Ava did a great job controlling the ball, then used an outside stepover to get around Charlie before kicking past Luka and into the back of the net.

They swapped positions. Charlie attacked with the ball next.

'The play I'm talking about is also something the Matildas are pretty good at,' Coach explained once Charlie had finished. 'Anyone?'

Controlling the ball and using good skills are especially important in the midfield, Sasha thought. *We also did a midfield drill on Monday.*

Sasha raised her hand. 'I think it's about

moving the ball through the midfield and trying to score.'

'It is indeed. Anything else?' Coach asked.

'Well, two of the Matildas attacking midfielders were hugely important during qualifying for the Olympics in 2020,' Sasha said. 'It was Caitlin Foord and Emily van Egmond and they both scored hat-tricks in that tournament.'

Sasha glanced towards the clubhouse, where Emily was standing that very minute.

'Well done, Sasha,' Coach said. 'A slushie for you.'

'Woof! Woof!'

'Thanks, Diego.' Sasha gave him a scratch between the eyes.

'Okay, quick water break, then you can get going on your video,' Coach said. 'I'm going to check how they're doing at the clubhouse. Diego, you're with me.'

Seeing Australian football stars at their oval had everyone fired up. Sasha was excited, but that wasn't what was making her nervous. She'd grabbed her short list of tricks. It was finally time to work out their plan.

Please let everyone agree.

Sasha had seen Finn's face during their drink break. He'd looked excited chatting with Hani. She'd thought it was because of Awer Mabil, but she now realised she'd been wrong. Finn had his own list: a list of skills.

How could he do this to me?

'So, Hani and I were thinking that doing some fun skills could be a way to include *everyone* in the video,' Finn said, before she could speak.

Sasha frowned, gripping her paper harder.

Was that a dig at me?

She looked at the faces of her teammates. Hani was smiling and nodding. So were Crabbie, Kat and Harper.

So, now everyone's ganging up on me?

'That's, um, that's great, Finn,' Sasha said, keeping her voice calm. 'But we did talk about how tricks look a bit more, well, impressive.' She couldn't look Finn in the eye. 'I've got a list too. I'm sure there's something here everyone can do. We don't have much time. Maybe we should just focus on this.'

'Sounds good,' Kyra said.

Sasha let out a breath.

'I'm keen for tricks,' Charlie said, nodding to Sasha.

Kat's ponytail whipped from side to side as she shook her head. 'I'd rather try Finn's idea.'

'Me too,' Crabbie said.

Everyone was silent. Sasha adjusted her headband. She saw Harper and Meili exchange a worried glance.

'How about we try both?' Harper said eventually. She tilted her head and pushed her glasses back on her nose.

'Great idea,' Meili said. She looked at Sasha, then at Finn. 'You could both run a session and we can see what works.'

Sasha tried to keep her breathing calm. They were wasting time!

'Sure,' Finn said. He didn't seem thrilled either, but they didn't have a choice.

'Okay,' Sasha said. Maybe this would help everyone see that she was right. She collected a few balls and watched Finn do the same. The rest of the Fever split up between them. In front of Sasha were Kyra and Charlie. She was pleased to see Kat, Harper and Crabbie there as well, willing to give her idea a try.

'What trick are we doing?' Harper asked.

'Why don't we choose together?' Sasha said.

They crowded around, looking at the list.

1. *Heel juggle*
2. *Around the world*
3. *Rainbow flick*
4. *Catch on foot*

'I want to try an around the world,' Crabbie said.

Charlie was grinning. 'Me too.'

‘That might be a bit hard for me.’ Harper scrunched up her nose. ‘Can I try heel juggling instead?’

‘I’m with Harper,’ Kat added.

‘Okay,’ Sasha said. ‘Kyra, can you help Harper and Kat? I’ll go with Crabbie and Charlie.’

Sasha looked over at Finn’s group. She saw him put one foot on top of the ball, drag it towards him, then spin and change direction – the perfect Maradona turn. She knew it wasn’t easy, but there was no way it was impressive enough to win them the Half-time Heroes competition. The muscles in her jaw twitched. It had to be tricks.

‘Okay. Crabbie, Charlie, let’s start with a *half* around the world,’ Sasha said. ‘You can both juggle off your toes, right?’

Charlie nodded.

Crabbie grimaced. 'Kind of.'

'Good enough.' Sasha gave her best encouraging smile. 'Just drop it lightly and try to use the toe box, this bit just in front of the laces.' She pointed at her boot. 'That will help the ball go up instead of out.'

They practised it a few times. Charlie was pretty good and, after a slow start, Crabbie improved quickly.

'Now, you're going to bounce it off your toes, then use the same foot to circle over the ball from the inside,' Sasha explained. 'To finish, bounce the ball on the toe of your other foot. Like this.'

She demonstrated, lightly tapping the ball before catching it to finish.

'And that's how you do a half around the world,' she said. She was pretty sure they would all get it now.

'Looks cool,' Charlie said.

They both gave it a go. Charlie was a natural, but Crabbie struggled to get his foot over without sending the ball flying. She left him to practise and turned to check in with Harper and Kat.

‘Where did they go?’ Sasha asked Kyra, who was now standing talking with Meili and Ava.

‘They wanted to try a few skills,’ Kyra said with a shrug.

‘And we wanted to come and try out some tricks,’ Ava added.

‘Great,’ Sasha said, but her stomach dropped. It wasn’t Ava and Meili she had to convince. She looked over at Crabbie. He was sitting on a ball, head in his hands.

‘Do you want to try a different trick?’ Sasha asked, walking towards him.

‘Nah,’ he said, standing back up. ‘I’m going to check out what Finn’s doing.’

As she watched Crabbie walk away, it felt like he was taking her Half-time Heroes dreams with him.

CHAPTER 7

Meili, Sam and Ava had been making good progress with the Maradona turn, so Finn was disappointed when they headed over to do tricks. He was happy to see Kat, Harper and Crabbie, though.

'I tried the half around the world,' Crabbie explained, shaking his head. 'I was hopeless.'

'I'm sure you weren't *that* bad,' Harper said, nudging him with her elbow.

Crabbie raised both his eyebrows. They all laughed.

'We've been working on the Maradona turn, but we were going to have a go at the Rabona,' Finn said. 'It's where you cross your leg behind your standing leg to kick the ball.'

'Awesome,' Kat said.

As they each grabbed a ball, Finn looked over to Sasha. Her group was practising rainbow flicks. They looked impressive. Finn frowned. The Fever was split in half, and it didn't feel right.

After ten minutes, Kat, Luka, Hani, Harper and Crabbie were all nailing the Maradona and the Rabona. They'd even done some Cruyff turns at speed.

They looked great, but so did everyone with Sasha.

‘Hey Fever,’ Coach called out. ‘How are you all going?’

Finn spun around and his heart started to race. Walking towards them with Coach and Old Noel was Awer Mabil and Emily van Egmond.

‘Hey there, Merridale Fever,’ Awer said.

‘Hi everyone,’ Emily added.

Finn felt frozen to the spot.

Is this really happening?

‘I hear you’re working out what to do for the Half-time Heroes video,’ Emily said with a smile. ‘Have you figured out how to show what makes your team special?’

Finn snuck a look at Sasha. She was staring at the ground, chewing the inside of her cheek.

‘How about you show us what you’ve

been practising?' Coach said, when no-one spoke.

The tricks group went first. Sasha looked as nervous as Finn felt as she lined up with Kyra, Ava, Meili, Sam and Charlie. They did the half around the world, one by one, then Sasha ended with a rainbow flick. Everyone clapped.

Finn's group stepped up next. Moving in a line, Finn, along with Crabbie, Kat,

Harper, Hani and Luka, ran forward. They all did a Maradona, then used a Rabona to shoot for goal.

As everyone clapped them, Finn glanced at Awer. His hero was smiling. It should have been an amazing moment, but it wasn't. He hadn't shared it with his best friend, or his whole team.

Finn stood quietly as Emily, Awer, Coach and Noel talked.

'You're all so talented,' Emily said, eventually. 'The skill needed for those tricks is huge.' Finn saw Sasha's cheeks go red.

'And all of you pulling off the Maradona and Rabona together like that is also seriously impressive,' Awer added. 'So, when you're deciding what to do, the important thing to remember is what this video is about.'

'That's right,' Emily said. 'What makes the Merridale Fever different to everyone else? What makes *your team* special?'

'Nail that, and you'll be Half-time Heroes for sure,' Awer said.

Emily smiled again. 'We have to go, but hopefully we'll see you all on the pitch very soon.'

Finn should have been happy, but he felt sick as he watched them walk away. He knew they were right.

What makes our team special? he thought as he looked at his friends. The truth was, he had no idea.

'Okay, everyone,' Coach said. 'Time to pack up.'

The Fever were unusually quiet as they piled balls into Coach's net bag and stacked the cones. Then they gathered their bags and stood looking at each other. No-one was smiling. Finn's whole body was tense. He knew how badly they all wanted to be Half-time Heroes and play at the Socceroos game. They had to sort this out.

'What are we going to do?' Meili eventually asked.

'Surely you could all see how cool the tricks looked,' Sasha said. 'Maybe the rest of you could stand opposite and catch when we flick?'

Catch when you flick? Finn thought. *Are you for real?*

'Didn't you hear what Emily said?' he snapped. He couldn't believe Sasha was being so stubborn. 'It needs to be about us *as a team*.'

Sasha's eyebrows were furrowed, and her arms crossed. He knew the look. She wasn't backing down, so neither would he.

'You can do a Rabona – right, Sasha?' Finn continued. 'So can pretty much everyone.' Finn tried to keep his voice steady. 'Skills mean we can *all* be part of the video. The whole team. Not only half of us.'

Sasha's face was red. She looked at Kyra.

'But tricks do look better, Finn,' Kyra said. She shrugged. 'Sorry, it's true.'

Finn crossed his arms too.

'Have you considered making the video about something *other* than tricks or skills?' Noel asked from behind.

Finn spun around. He hadn't seen Noel and Coach walk back over. Finn wished he could disappear into a big hole.

Old Noel shrugged. 'Food for thought,' he said. 'Now, speaking of food . . .'

Noel winked as he grabbed the bag of balls and wandered back towards the clubhouse.

'Noel's right,' Coach said. 'You have a game on Saturday and not a lot of time left to get this video done. Maybe come up with some different ideas and be ready to decide then.'

Finn walked slowly to the car park, head down. He wasn't sure what different ideas there could be, but Coach was right about one thing. Time was running out.

CHAPTER 8

Saturday. Game Day. Sasha was in her Merridale FC yellow and green jersey. Normally being in club colours was the best feeling ever – sometimes she imagined it was the Matildas green-and-gold – but today, nothing felt right. Her football boots were uncomfortable, she was frustrated about the video and she was annoyed with Finn. She'd never been upset with him before, and she didn't like it.

If he'd just agreed to tricks, we'd have the video done by now.

They still hadn't messaged or spoken. When she was worried, hanging out with Finn usually made her feel better. She missed him.

Deep breath in. Hold. Slowly breathe out.

'You're on Field 1,' her dad said. They were standing outside the clubhouse.

'Thanks, Dad.' She picked up her backpack. 'See you after, I guess.'

'You okay, Sasha?' Dad asked.

'Yeah,' she said, forcing a smile. 'I'm just a bit tired.'

Dad raised one eyebrow. 'If you say so,' he said. 'Have a good game.'

Sasha's stomach was in knots as she walked up to her team. Normally everyone stood together, chatting. Today, there were two clear groups: tricks and skills. The knots twisted tighter.

Harper and Meili were the only exceptions. They were standing in the middle. Harper's eyebrows were pinched together and Meili was frowning. Meili rarely frowned.

Sasha put her bag down and stood beside Kyra. She took another breath.

It will be okay.

The Fever did their normal pre-game warm-up, but it didn't feel normal. When Ava fell over doing leg swings, Luka rolled his eyes instead of laughing. Charlie got grumpy with Hani when they bumped into each other. Not even Diego's antics could make anyone smile.

'Okay, Fever,' Coach said as they huddled around. 'I'm not sure what's going on, but whatever it is, you need to forget it for the next fifty minutes.' She looked at each of them in turn. 'It's game time. Timbervale FC is tough. I need you to focus and show me that Fever magic. Got it?'

'Yes, Coach,' they all replied, more quietly than usual.

Coach ran through their starting positions. Kyra, Crabbie and Ava were on the bench.

'Right,' Coach said. 'Hands in.'

Sasha looked at Finn. He wouldn't meet her eye.

'FEVER TIME!' they called out, louder this time.

Sasha was next to Finn as they jogged onto the pitch. He felt so far away. She couldn't stand it. She decided to be brave.

'Have a good game,' she said.

'You too,' he replied.

Their eyes met for a second, then they both looked away. It felt like they were strangers, not best friends. Sasha watched Finn run past Hani and laugh at something he said. Sasha chewed the inside of her lip. *She* was usually the one he laughed with like that. Sasha huffed out a breath. She couldn't think about it now. Coach was right. They had a game to play, and she had the kick-off.

Brrrp!

Normally Sasha would pass to Hani, her partner in the midfield. But when she saw Sam running up, she passed to him instead. At least Sam was supporting her. Sam passed to Charlie, who was quickly surrounded. Sasha followed the play up the sideline towards their goal. Hani called out. He was in the clear. Sasha called out too. Charlie passed to her, and

Hani shook his head. He'd been the better choice. He knew it and so did Sasha. But Charlie was on her side. She'd barely touched the ball when she was tackled by a Timbervale player. Sasha grunted as she used an outside turn to get past, but another player was waiting. Sasha saw Finn fake and race clear, calling for the pass. He was in a good position. She took precious seconds to look around. Sam was also moving towards her. It was a harder pass. She chose Sam, but she'd taken too long. A Timbervale player intercepted and raced towards his goal. Harper, Luka and Kat fought hard, but the Timbervale attacker was too good. Two more quick passes and a girl sent the ball low and fast into the corner of the net, despite Meili's best efforts to block it. Only minutes in, the Fever were 0–1 down.

Sasha stared at the ground. Her cheeks were red, and not just from running. She should have passed to Finn. That goal was her fault.

Hani had the next kick-off. Instead of pushing the ball to Sasha, he passed to Harper. Harper looked surprised but recovered and moved the ball forward before passing back to Hani. He slid the ball straight on to Finn. Sasha was calling out, so were Charlie and Sam, but Finn ignored them, his eyes searching for someone else. Sasha could see Finn struggling to get around a Timbervale defender. He needed to pass. He didn't. He tried a Cruyff turn, but the ball spun straight to the foot of a Timbervale player, who took off at top speed towards her goal. Harper was a head shorter than the girl, but she didn't hesitate. Sasha's boots felt superglued to the grass as she watched her friend race in front, a determined look on her face.

Sasha wasn't sure exactly what happened next, but she didn't miss the tangle of legs or Harper's cry as she crashed to the ground.

CHAPTER 9

Finn stared down the pitch in horror. Harper was lying on the ground clutching her arm to her chest and she wasn't getting up.

The referee blew his whistle to pause the game and Coach raced to Harper's side. Finn saw Harper's shoulders shaking as Coach spoke quietly, rubbing her back. He looked around. Everyone wore identical worried expressions, both Fever and Timbervale players. Coach handed

Harper her glasses and slowly helped her stand. Harper's face was white, and she was cradling her arm. She gave her teammates a shaky smile as Coach guided her to the sideline and her parents.

Finn looked at Sasha. Her eyes were glistening. They'd both been so stubborn. Now their friend was hurt.

Coach was talking to Ava, Crabbie and Kyra. Finn was sure he'd be taken off. Instead, Crabbie replaced Meili in goals, while Kyra waved Charlie to the sideline and Ava took Harper's place in defence.

Timbervale had the ball to restart.

'Stay focused, Fever,' Coach called out. 'Harper's okay. You can do this.'

As Finn jogged into position, he looked at Sasha. Her forehead was crinkled and her lips were pressed together. He could see that she was ready to fight back. They all were, for Harper. For the rest of the match, the Fever played in unison. The perfect team. The final score was 5–4.

The Fever had won, but Finn just felt sad.

*

Sitting in the Fever Creek House, Finn watched his teammates speak in hushed voices. Diego lay quietly at Kyra's feet, head between his paws. It reminded Finn of the time Kyra didn't invite Sam to the creek house after their first training session. It felt wrong. Finn knew they were all worried about Harper. Her parents had taken her to the hospital for an X-ray. Harper wasn't very big, but the hole she left was huge. He also knew the problem wasn't just Harper getting hurt.

Finn glanced up at the sound of thunder. A storm was on its way. Finn cleared his throat. The creek house fell silent. His eyes darted towards Sasha. She was standing in the corner on her own. She looked miserable.

'I don't know how it happened,' Finn said. 'But this video . . .' His voice trailed off and he picked at a loose bit of timber on the table beside him. 'I'm sorry if I made anyone feel like they had to take sides.'

'I'm sorry too,' Sasha said. She came to stand beside Finn. 'I was so stuck on tricks as the only idea for the video, I wouldn't listen to any other ideas.'

Finn gave her a small smile. She smiled back.

'It wasn't just you two,' Kat said. 'We all took sides.'

'Yeah, we did,' Kyra agreed.

'It felt awful,' Ava said. 'Being a Half-time Hero is just such a big deal.'

'And at a Socceroos match too,' Luka added. 'It's just . . . *huge*.'

'It sure is,' Sam said, leaning forward in his chair. 'But splitting in half isn't going to get us there. We have to figure out what makes our *whole* team special.'

'And show that in a video,' Crabbie said, then the creek house fell silent again.

Finn's mind was going in circles.

We're the Merridale Fever.

We've won every game.

We've been together for years and we all want to play for Australia some day.

But what makes us special?

They all jumped at the sound of knocking on the creek house door.

Then, Old Noel stuck his head inside. He wore a green Merridale raincoat and was red-faced and puffing.

'Did you have to make this creek house

so far away?' he asked. His voice was gruff, but Finn could see the twinkle in his eye. 'Anyhoo, you lot need to come back to the clubhouse. There's a big storm on the way and it's coming faster than we expected.'

'Um, our parents won't be back for a while,' Kat said. 'Is that okay?'

'Of course. You can help me put back all the stuff I had to drag out for those videos they were shooting the other day.' Noel grinned. 'I've got plenty to fill in your time.'

'But our video,' Kyra said. 'We still haven't figured it out.'

'You might find some inspiration at the clubhouse,' Noel said. He glanced outside at the sky. 'Come on. Let's get moving.'

The Fever grabbed their bags. As they hurried towards the creek, Finn felt big, fat raindrops fall on his arms and head. He followed Diego, Old Noel and his teammates across the stones and up the embankment to the oval. They were still a few metres from the clubhouse when the rain came hammering down. They raced inside, laughing and soaked.

'Dry yourselves off, then it's time to get to work,' Noel said, pointing at some towels on a shelf.

Finn looked at the old football stuff lying all around them. There were piles of newspapers and boxes filled with football memorabilia: banners, trophies and lots of photos. It was the history of Merridale FC. Finn crouched down for a closer look, wondering what he would find. Old Noel seemed confident the answer to their Half-time Heroes question would be somewhere in these boxes. Finn took a deep breath.

I hope he's right.

CHAPTER 10

Sasha couldn't stop the corner of her mouth twitching up as Hani kept up a steady stream of chatter. Sorting through all this old stuff was clearly his dream afternoon.

'Did you know Merridale's uniform used to be green and yellow stripes?' Hani asked. 'See!' He held up a striped banner with the Merridale tree motif in the middle. 'This is so cool.'

'I suppose you can tell us when it changed too,' Sasha said with a laugh.

'Actually, I can.' Hani grinned and held up a Merridale FC brochure. 'It was in 1976 the club changed the design to what we have today,' he read.

'I remember it well,' Noel called out from the kitchen. 'Very nice, Master Hani.'

'Don't tell me, he gets *another* slushie!' Crabbie fake groaned, then groaned again as suddenly Diego appeared and tried to cover him in sloppy licks.

'The answer for our video is here. I can feel it,' Sasha said, placing another old newspaper in a box. 'It has to be.'

'But what if it's not?' Meili asked. 'I *really* want us to be Half-time Heroes.'

'We *will* be,' Kyra told her. 'We just need to look at it from a different angle.'

They all laughed as Kyra kicked up into a handstand against the wall.

'Kyra's right,' Finn said. 'We're going to figure it out.'

'OMG,' Hani said, holding up another photograph. 'Check it out.'

The Fever crowded around. It was a grainy photo of a Merridale team from long ago. Sasha's eyes went straight to a young man in the centre of the picture. He was holding the Merridale Cup high above his head. Sasha was impressed. The whole club could nominate teams for the Cup each season, and the Committee made the final decision. It wasn't just how well you played, but how much you gave to the club and football.

Sasha looked closer. 'That has to be Noel,' she said excitedly. 'Right?'

'For sure,' Finn replied.

'He looks so young,' Ava said. 'How cool is it that he won the Cup!'

'It *was* "cool" as you say, young Ava,' Noel said, stepping out of the kitchen. He took the photo and sat on a chair. 'But *I* didn't win it, our *team* did.' Noel squinted at the picture. 'Actually, there's someone there you may have heard of.' He pointed at the picture. 'Harry Williams. That was 1970. So, four years after that game, Harry became the first Indigenous Australian player to wear the green-and-gold.' Noel chuckled. 'Gosh, we were a crazy bunch. We had a couple of really fast guys, and another one who could do all those fancy turns you lot practise. We were all so different, but somehow the team just worked.'

So different.

Sasha looked around at her teammates.

When she'd started playing football she wasn't fitting in at school. There were too many questions about her 'different' family and why she didn't like all the stuff other girls liked. Then she'd joined the Fever. She'd found her place and her dream.

'Were you captain?' Hani asked.

Noel nodded. 'Yes. For some reason these guys decided I should be the one to keep them in line.' Noel chuckled again. 'Can you read what that says down the bottom?'

Sasha leaned in as he held up the photo.

'No way,' she said.

'Yes way,' Noel said, grinning.

'What?' Finn asked.

'The team's name was Merridale Fever,' Sasha said.

Everyone started talking at once.

‘Hey kiddos.’ Sam’s dad, Jason Elrick, knocked on the wall beside the door, breaking through the excited chatter.

‘Hey Dad,’ Sam said. ‘Did you know Noel’s old team from, like, a hundred years ago was the Merridale Fever too?’

‘A hundred years might be a bit of an exaggeration,’ Mr Elrick said. ‘But that’s very cool.’ He looked towards Noel. ‘Thanks for keeping an eye on them.’

‘No problem.’

‘Luka, Kat and Kyra, you guys are coming with me,’ Mr Elrick said.

‘Woof!’

‘Yes, you too, Diego,’ he laughed. ‘There’s a nice big boot for you to ride in.’

All the other parents were arriving as well. Sasha’s phone pinged.

‘Uh, Noel,’ she said. ‘Paps is running fifteen minutes late. Is that okay?’

'No problem at all, young lady,' Noel said. 'And what about you, Master Finn?'

'Well, um, Paps said he's picking Finn up too,' Sasha replied, glancing sideways at her friend.

'Cool,' Finn said with a smile. Sasha let out a breath.

'Keep thinking,' Sasha said to her other teammates as they grabbed their bags and headed to the door. 'Let's message each other with video ideas. We need to record it on Monday. We *have* to be the Half-time Heroes!'

There was plenty of noise and laughter as the others headed out into the rain. Sasha still wasn't sure what they were going to do, but now they were a team again, she was more hopeful they could figure it out.

Sasha and Finn got back to work as Noel

disappeared again. Most of the boxes were sorted now, so they started carrying them out to the storeroom.

'Oof,' Sasha said, walking straight into Finn, who had stopped in the doorway. 'What are you . . .'

Her voice trailed off as she stared, mouth open, at the two people standing at the clubhouse door. Shaking rain off a couple of Football Australia umbrellas was Emily van Egmond and Awer Mabil.

CHAPTER 11

'Hello there,' Awer said. 'Is Noel around?'

Finn nodded. 'Um, yeah.' He cleared his throat. 'He's –'

'I forgot you two were stopping by,' Noel said, coming out of the kitchen. He winked at Finn and Sasha. Finn was pretty sure he hadn't forgotten. He silently thanked Mr Parry for running late!

'Sorry, the traffic was a bit heavy in the rain,' said Emily.

'No trouble. I've got all your things in the kitchen,' Noel said. 'I'll just go and sort them out for you.'

'Thanks, Noel,' Awer said.

'How are you guys going?' Emily asked, coming over to where the last boxes were piled up.

'Um, good, thanks,' Sasha said, finally finding her voice.

'We've been helping Noel put this stuff away,' Finn added. He gave himself a mental forehead slap. *Helping put stuff away? So lame.*

'Would you like a hand?' Awer asked.

Finn looked at Sasha. She seemed as excited as he felt.

'Yeah, thanks,' Finn said.

'How about I help you finish packing up those newspapers,' Emily said to Sasha.

'And we can get these boxes out of the

way,' Awer said to Finn. They picked up a box each and headed into the storeroom. Finn wanted to pinch himself to be sure this was really happening, but his hands were full.

'How was your game today?' Awer asked.

'Yeah, good,' Finn said, then his smile faded. 'Sort of.'

'Sort of?'

'Yeah. Well, no. It wasn't so great. We won, but my teammate Harper got hurt.' He looked down. 'I feel like it was kind of my fault.'

'Do you want to talk about it?' Awer asked.

Finn felt confused. He wanted to impress Awer, but he also wanted to be honest. 'You know that video we need to do?' he said eventually.

‘Sure,’ Awer said. ‘You had some mean skills when you showed us that Maradona and Rabona.’

Finn managed half a smile. ‘Thanks. But remember some of the Fever showed off tricks too?’

Awer nodded. ‘They were great as well.’

‘That’s the problem,’ Finn explained. ‘We’re all good at things, just not the same thing. We couldn’t agree and we kind of, um, weren’t playing the best as a team today.’

Awer sat on a box and patted the space beside him. Finn sat down.

‘Do you remember when I kicked that penalty at the World Cup qualifier?’ Awer asked.

‘Of course,’ Finn said. ‘It was incredible.’

‘Thanks. Do you know what I loved the most about that moment?’

Finn shook his head.

'We were tied at four-all,' Awer said. 'It was sudden death, and I was kicking to get us into the World Cup. I *had* to score, not just for the World Cup, but because I wanted to say thank you to Australia for taking my family in.' Awer smiled. 'I was given that chance because of who I am. There's no-one else in the Socceroos like me. Not because of where I was born or how I came to Australia, but because every one of us is different. We all have different skills. It's when you put them together –'

'– that the team just works,' Finn said quietly, echoing Old Noel's words.

Awer nodded and smiled. 'Yes.'

'That's why Andrew Redmayne came on for Mat Ryan just before the penalty kicks too, isn't it?' Finn asked. 'Crabbie, our goalkeeper, said he's a spot-kick specialist.'

'Yes, and that's why Mat supported that call,' Awer said. 'He's our captain, and he came off the field because he knows what Andrew's strengths are – and they were what we needed in that moment.'

Finn took a deep breath. An idea was forming in his mind. 'Thanks, Awer,' he said. 'That really helps.'

Awer stood up. 'My pleasure. I reckon we can get the rest of the boxes in if we're quick. What do you think?'

Finn nodded and followed Awer out of the storeroom. He could see Sasha and Emily sitting on the floor next to the pile of old newspapers. They were deep in conversation. He smiled. He knew how excited Sasha must be right now talking to her hero. Finn was excited too. He finally had a plan for their Half-time Heroes video, and he couldn't wait to tell his best friend.

CHAPTER 12

Sasha couldn't believe it. Her whole body was tingling. Sitting next to her, in the Merridale FC clubhouse, was Emily van Egmond!

'That rainbow flick you did the other day was very impressive,' Emily said as she folded a newspaper and placed it in a box.

'Thanks. I love watching you play,' Sasha gushed. 'I've seen your 2020 Olympic qualifying matches so many times.

Especially the one against Thailand. A hat-trick! And you created, like, eight chances. Or that chipped reverse pass with the outside of your foot before Steph Catley scored against Taiwan.' Sasha slapped her hand over her mouth. 'Sorry, I'm talking way too much, right?'

Emily laughed. 'No, not at all. They *were* special games. I get excited thinking about them too. Do you play midfield?'

'Yep,' Sasha said. 'I want to play in the number 10 spot too one day, for the Matildas.'

'Perhaps you will,' Emily said. 'If you win that Half-time Heroes competition, you could be running out at Accor Stadium very soon.'

Sasha's smile faded. 'Yeah, maybe.'

'You don't sound very excited,' Emily said.

Sasha sighed. 'We're still having trouble figuring out what makes our team special.'

Emily put down a newspaper. 'What seems to be the problem?'

Sasha looked at the newspaper in her hand, taking a moment to think. 'Well, when we split into two groups at training,' she said, 'it wasn't because we wanted to show you everything we could do. It was because we couldn't agree what to do.' Sasha put a newspaper into the box, keeping her eyes down. 'Trying to work out what made our team special, split us in half.'

'That's tough,' Emily said.

'Yeah, and because we weren't being a good team, our friend got hurt in the game today.' Sasha felt a lump in her throat. 'We know we went about it all wrong, but we still don't know what to do.' A tear rolled down her cheek. She quickly wiped it away.

'Do you know what I love the most about the CommBank Matildas?' Emily asked gently. Sasha shook her head. 'It's that we don't try to be the same. Caitlin, Kyra, Mary, Sam . . . they're all incredible up forward, but it's Lydia, Teagan and Mackenzie who shine in goal. It's the same for Ellie, Alanna, Charlotte and all the girls in defence, or Aivi, Clare and Tameka with me in the midfield.' Emily smiled. 'Don't get me started on some of our newer Matildas, like Princess Ibini-Isei. Sasha, don't be afraid to celebrate the things that make you different,' Emily continued. 'It would be very boring if we were all the same, all the time.'

Celebrate being different. Her football friends *and* her family.

'Old Noel said something like that too,' Sasha said.

'Old Noel is very wise.' Emily smiled. 'Sasha, you Fever kids are amazing players. Your coach believes you all have the potential to play for Australia one day. So, don't give up. Believe in yourselves, and get that video done. I'd love to see you as Half-time Heroes. Okay?'

'Okay,' Sasha said. She gave Emily a hug. 'Thank you.'

'It's my pleasure,' Emily said. She picked up the last pile of newspapers and put them in the box.

'Nice work, you lot,' Noel said. He was carrying two full Merridale FC sports bags and handed them to Awer and Emily.

'Thanks, Noel,' Emily said.

'Yeah, thanks,' Awer said. 'Maybe next time we can get one of those famous Noel sausage sandwiches Joel keeps telling me about!'

'Or a mixed-flavour slushie,' Emily said. 'I hear they're pretty good.'

Noel laughed. 'Perhaps. If you both behave yourselves.'

'Good luck with the video, guys,' Emily said.

'You're going to nail it,' Awer added.

Sasha and Finn watched their heroes head out into the rain.

'I've got an –' Sasha started.

'I think I know –' Finn said at the same time.

They both grinned.

'You first,' Finn said.

'I figured out where we were going wrong,' Sasha said excitedly. 'I thought we had to find *one* thing that made our team special. It was never going to work – and that's the whole point.'

'Exactly,' he said. 'We're all good at different things.'

'And *that's* what makes our team special,' they finished together.

'I know what we have to do,' Sasha said. She pulled out her phone. With Finn making a few suggestions, she typed out a message. Finn nodded. Sasha hit send.

CHAPTER 13

'Do you really think this is going to work?' Sasha was pacing and adjusting her headband for the kazillionth time.

'I *know* it will, and so do you,' Finn said. 'Remember Harper's reaction yesterday?'

Sasha stopped pacing and smiled. 'Yeah, she seemed pretty excited.'

Finn and Sasha had gone to check on Harper. Luckily her arm wasn't broken, it was just sprained and bruised. The doctor said she had to keep it strapped and in a sling for a bit, but she'd probably only miss one week of football. Her parents had agreed to let her be part of the Half-time Heroes video, though, as long as she was careful.

Coach had also agreed to give the team Monday's training time to film. Now they were at Merridale Oval, ready to go. Finn twisted his hair up into a bun.

'Okay, Sasha and Finn,' Coach said. 'You're in charge.'

'Thanks, Coach,' Finn said, then looked around his teammates. 'I know it was a bit of a random message we sent you all, but Sasha and I realised we'd been thinking about the Half-time Heroes video all wrong.'

'We never needed to find one thing we could *all* do,' Sasha explained. 'The Fever is special because of all the *different* things we can do.'

Finn smiled at Sasha. 'So, using what you all sent, we've come up with an idea.'

'What do you have in mind?' Kyra asked.

Finn took a deep breath. 'Sasha and I thought we'd film you one at a time. You get passed the ball, you say who inspires you, do your favourite football thing, then pass the ball out of shot,' he said. 'Then we'll edit them all together.'

'And I thought the last pass could be to Diego,' Harper said. 'After all, he *is* our ball dog and he's definitely part of the team.'

'It was a brilliant idea,' Sasha said. 'And Kyra, your idea was great too. Did you make it?'

'I sure did.' Kyra made Diego sit while she slipped a modified Merridale jersey over his head. 'Number 10 for the legend Diego Maradona, of course.'

‘Woof!’ Diego grinned.

Meili raised her hand. ‘Maybe when Diego gets the ball, we can all crowd in for one final cheer,’ she said.

Finn nodded. ‘Perfect.’

‘It sounds like you’ve got a great plan,’ Coach said. ‘I’m proud of you all. I know this hasn’t been easy.’

Finn could hear everyone sharing their ideas as they finished getting ready. He went over to Old Noel, who had agreed to be their cameraman.

‘It’s all set up, so you just have to hit record when each of us is ready,’ Finn explained.

‘Not a problem, Master Finn.’ Noel sat on a bench behind the tripod.

‘Okay, everyone,’ Finn said as he stood beside Sasha, who was gripping her phone. ‘Here’s the order. What do you think?’

Name	Football Hero	Trick or Skill
Kyra	Mary Fowler	Catch on foot
Hani	Ajdin Hrustic	Rabona
Ava	Charlotte Grant	Neck stall
Sam	Joel King	Cruyff turn and kick at goal
Crabbie	Andrew Redmayne	Diving W
Kat	Courtney Nevin	Ronaldo
Charlie	Marco Tilio	Round the world
Luka	Milos Degenek	Cruyff turn
Meili	Lydia Williams	Scoop and throw
Harper	Kyah Simon	Fast dribble
Sasha	Emily van Egmond	Rainbow flick
Finn	Awer Mabil	Maradona
Diego – round up ball		
Fever group cheer		

'Kyra, are you okay to go first?' Sasha asked, glancing down at her phone.

'You bet!' Kyra said.

Crabbie was bouncing around on his toes. 'This is so awesome,' he said.

'Okay,' Sasha said. 'Let's do this!'

They all lined up.

'Ready, Noel?' Finn asked.

Old Noel gave him a thumbs up. 'Aaaaaand ACTION!'

'Hi. I'm Kyra, and Mary Fowler is my inspiration,' she said to the camera.

Finn stood to the side watching his teammates as they stepped up one by one. He was smiling so hard his cheeks were hurting. It was better than he had imagined. There were tricks *and* skills, and they were all so good. Sam and Crabbie teamed up for their bit: after Sam's Cruyff turn, Crabbie saved his goal attempt. Finally, Sasha stepped in front of the camera.

'My name is Sasha. Emily van Egmond is my hero,' she said. 'She taught me we shouldn't all try to be the same. We need to celebrate the things that make us different.'

Sasha performed a perfect rainbow flick, then it was Finn's turn.

'I'm Finn. The player who inspires me is Awer Mabil,' he said. 'He taught me it's our *different* strengths that makes us special as a team.' Finn took a couple of steps then, using a Maradona, turned and sent the ball off to the side.

Finally, Diego rounded up a ball and delivered it back to the team. They huddled together, looking at the camera.

'We're the Merridale Fever Under 11s and we'd love to be Half-time Heroes,' Sasha said.

'What makes our team special?' Finn asked.

'*We* do,' everyone answered together.

'Woof!'

CHAPTER 14

Sasha was excited to be back in her Merridale game-day jersey. They had an away game, against Brolstan FC. It was going to be tough. Thursday training had been cancelled because of severe rain, so this was the first time the Fever had been together since they'd filmed their parts for the Half-time Heroes competition.

'You and Finn did such an awesome job with the video,' Harper said. She had a sling on over her Merridale FC jacket.

She'd insisted on coming to cheer on the Fever even if she couldn't play.

'Thanks,' Sasha said. 'It was so much fun!'

She'd gone to Finn's house after training on Monday. Everything had been back to normal. It was like the whole not-talking thing had never happened. They'd cut the video together and added music and some cool transitions, and sent it off. Sasha had also solved her school-project problem. Instead of worrying that her family wasn't like everyone else, she'd taken Emily's advice to celebrate what made them different. Finn helped by taking photos of her with her dads and her dragon, showing the fun and silly things they did together.

'Any idea when we find out about Half-time Heroes?' Crabbie asked, dumping his bag.

'I'm not sure. Although it's got to be soon,' Sasha replied.

'Hi everyone.'

Sasha turned and burst into laughter. It was Finn who had spoken but beside him was his little brother, Xavier, covered head to toe in mud.

'Good game, Xav?' Crabbie asked, with mock seriousness.

'Mhmm,' Xavier replied. 'It's a bit muddy, though.'

'No kidding,' Crabbie said, a laugh finally escaping. Xavier grinned back, his teeth white against his mud-splattered face.

Sasha laughed too. 'Did you like the video, Xav?' she asked.

'Oh yeah. You're going to be Half-time Heroes for sure,' Xavier said. 'Dad said I could go, and even Mum thinks she'll be able to watch. How cool is that!'

‘Very cool,’ Finn said. ‘Xav, I’ve got to get ready. Dad’s at the canteen.’

‘Yay,’ Xavier said. ‘I’m starving.’

‘Time to go,’ Coach said, calling the team together. As they ran through their warm-up and the game plan, Sasha could feel the energy. Everyone was so happy. This was going to be an epic game.

Brolstan had the kick-off, but the Fever were pumped. Only one Brolstan player managed a touch before Kat intercepted, spun and raced down the sideline towards the Fever’s goal. Sasha sprinted down the opposite side. Kat slipped, but got her footing back quickly. She passed to Finn, who sent the ball across the penalty box to Kyra. She slammed it straight into the back corner of the net. A goal!

Sasha felt so full inside. This was her team. The Fever.

Brolstan had the restart and were more careful, avoiding long passes and keeping the ball close to their feet. A lot more tackling meant a lot more falling over on the slippery pitch. It wasn't long before

the Brolstan *and* Fever players had a new jersey colour – brown! Crabbie looked like he'd been painted with mud, with all the diving and rolling around goal. Sasha was sure she didn't look much better.

All the players from both sides were cheering each other and laughing as they slipped and slid. Sasha had never played a game like it, and she'd never had so much fun. Coach gave up trying to do any real coaching, she was laughing too much. Brolstan's coach was the same. Despite the conditions, the Fever played really well. They ended up with three goals, two to Kyra and one to Finn. Brolstan scored three too. A fitting result.

'Woof! Woof!'

'Oh no, Diego,' Kyra said. They'd just gathered for a post-game chat.

Sasha turned and laughed. Diego looked so proud of himself, his tongue hanging out the side. But just like the Fever, his number 10 jersey – and all the fur around it – was black.

‘Anyone want a dog? Going free,’ Coach muttered, but Sasha saw the corner of her mouth twitch up as Diego turned his goofy grin her way.

Coach looked around their circle. ‘Despite the tough conditions, I think that was one of your best games,’ she said. ‘You worked so well as a team and played to your individual strengths. I’m proud of you all.’

Sasha joined her team dishing out muddy hugs and high-fives.

Coach smiled. ‘I just hope you’ll play that well at Accor Stadium next month.’

Sasha heard the words, but her brain struggled to understand them.

‘Um, pardon?’ Sasha squeaked out.

‘I said, I hope you play that well at Accor Stadium, when you run out as Half-time Heroes. You did it, kids,’ Coach said. ‘I got an email this morning. You're playing at the Socceroos game.'

Sasha could hear the chaos around her, but she couldn't move. Her heart was beating so hard she thought it might burst. She looked at Finn. He was grinning at her. She smiled back. They'd done it.

'Team hug!' Crabbie called out.

The Fever formed a circle, muddy arms wrapped around muddy shoulders. An equally mud-covered Diego sat happily in the middle.

'Woof! Woof! Woof!'

Sasha laughed. She couldn't have said it better herself.

CHAPTER 15

Four Weeks Later

Finn didn't think his life could feel more perfect. They were finally here, at Accor Stadium.

'Can you believe we're about to play an actual game out there?' Sasha said, echoing his thoughts.

Finn looked behind him. The Fever were lined up, all grinning in their Merridale game-day jerseys. The night had already been incredible, and they hadn't even played yet.

The bus had dropped them at an underground entrance, and they'd walked through the same grey walled tunnel the players used.

Imagine being here as a Socceroo!

Finn promised himself, one day he would. There was so much energy. People were rushing everywhere. There were TV sports commentators, and lots of people wearing green-and-gold. They looked like physios or trainers – all very official. He even thought he caught a glimpse of Awer Mabil as they passed an open door. Then came another surprise. Waiting for them in their meeting room was Emily van Egmond and CommBank Matildas goalkeeper Lydia Williams. Not only were they sitting with the Fever for the game, but they would coach them for their Half-time Heroes match.

Once the team had dropped their gear, Lydia and Emily had led them up into the stadium. The noise had hit him first: the hum of more than 80,000 people. A sell-out crowd. Finn thought they'd be in normal seats, but they were led into a VIP box. The first person Finn saw was his mum, wearing a green-and-gold headscarf and a huge smile. His dad and Xavier were sitting beside her. Earlier that week she'd been given the news the chemo had worked.

The Socceroos were playing a friendly against the USA. The first half was so close. Finn's heart had raced as he watched the teams dribble, tackle and race up and down the pitch. He had almost lost his voice screaming his support. The

Socceroos scored just before half-time when a brilliant assist by Awer Mabil set Jamie Maclaren up for a goal. By then, the Fever had already been in the tunnel warming up. They'd seen it on a monitor, and the crowd's roar had shaken the walls.

'This is it,' Emily said. 'Time to go.'

Finn's stomach was doing somersaults as they ran out of the tunnel and onto the

pitch. Huge floodlights lit up the stadium. Finn felt like he was standing in a spotlight. He looked at the crowd. It was a sea of green-and-gold. Somewhere up there was his family: Xavier, his dad *and* his mum. He could hardly believe it. Just a month ago he'd thought he'd lost his best friend and had no idea if his mum would be okay.

This is the best day ever!

'Right, team, gather around,' Lydia said. 'The game goes for ten minutes. Emily will call the subs, so keep an eye out for that.'

'Meili, we're going to start you in goal,' Lydia said. Finn saw Meili's cheeks turn a deep crimson as she grinned at the Matildas star goalie.

Emily looked at a piece of paper. 'Kyra, Sam, Finn, you're up front. Sasha and Hani, midfield. Kat, Luka and Harper, you'll start in defence.' She nodded to

Harper. 'Let us know if your arm's giving you any trouble, okay?'

Harper nodded. She had a wrist brace on but insisted it wasn't hurting much anymore.

'Hands in,' Lydia said. Then she looked at them all, one by one. 'There are a lot of people here, but remember to play the way you always do.'

'You're an amazing team,' Emily added, adding her hand to the pile. 'You've got this!'

'FEVER TIME!' they called out together.

Finn felt like all 80,000 sets of eyes were watching as he jogged to his spot up forward. Their opponents, Astonfield FC, had come from country New South Wales. They had Matildas stars Teagan Micah and Clare Polkinghorne helping them out. Finn's grin spread wider as he realised their referee was another football legend,

Matildas forward Kyah Simon. Astonfield had the kick-off.

Brrrp!

Finn's heart was pounding as he shot off his mark, racing towards the midfield. He saw Sasha run forward, tackling her much taller Astonfield opponent. Then, somehow, she had the ball.

Hani called out as Sasha turned the play, dribbling towards the Fever's goal. She faked to the right, then cut the ball past an Astonfield player before passing to Hani. He used an outside foot turn to dodge a defender, then sent the ball down the sideline to Sam. Sam immediately passed to Kyra, who was tackled by two Astonfield kids. Finn watched in awe. Their opponents were so good. Two against one, a boy stole the ball back and charged towards Astonfield's goal. Then

Luka was there. The boy passed. Kat tackled the next player, putting pressure on her. The Astonfield girl had a choice: pass or shoot. She tried for goal.

Finn held his breath, then let it out with a whoosh as Meili stopped the ball easily, scooping it up and throwing quickly to Harper, who raced back towards the Fever's end. Harper was so fast, she quickly left her Astonfield opponent behind, dribbling through the midfield. Then using her signature move, an outside touch, Harper dodged a defender and passed to Kyra, who booted the ball straight to Sam.

Finn saw Sam nod his way, so he pumped his arms and sprinted into the penalty box. Sam passed. The ball went straight to Finn's boot. He kicked hard. The ball slammed into the corner of the net.

Finn was stunned. He'd done it. A goal!

CHAPTER 16

Goooaaallll!

Sasha punched her fist in the air. Her best friend had just scored the first goal of their game at Accor Stadium. She wanted to give him a hug, but she had to stay focused. There would be time to celebrate later.

Sasha looked towards Emily as she jogged back to her starting position. Charlie raced on for Sam, and Ava replaced Luka.

Brrrp!

Astonfield kicked off again. This time Ava charged in, tackling her opponent, forcing her to pass. Sasha stayed with her player as they raced up the sideline. She saw the ball heading their way. Sprinting hard, she intercepted. The ball was hers.

Stay low, arms out, protect the ball.

Sasha could hear her own breath as she ran towards their goal. She could also hear her Astonfield defender puffing off her right shoulder. Sasha cut the ball across and moved to the left. She saw Charlie shift into position. She passed him the ball, but he was quickly brought up short by two Astonfield defenders. Sasha saw him fake, then pass to Finn, who fired the ball straight to Kyra. She kicked for goal. The Astonfield goalkeeper dived.

Yes!

The ball landed clean into the back of the net. Another goal to Merridale. The cheer from the crowd was deafening.

‘That’s halfway,’ Kyah called out as they reset. ‘Five minutes to go.’

Sasha saw Luka race on for Harper. Sam replaced Finn, and Crabbie moved into goal. Lydia gave Meili a high-five as she reached the sideline. A huge grin was stretched across the tiny goalkeeper’s face.

Brrrp!

Astonfield was clearly determined to score, and they threw everything at the Fever. Luka, Kat and Ava were fighting hard, but Astonfield was tough in attack, sidestepping and dodging. Despite some rock-solid defence, an Astonfield striker broke through. Crabbie dived. The ball just slipped past his fingers.

It was an impressive goal.

Emily called Sasha to sub off, and Harper ran back onto the pitch.

‘That was great football, Sasha,’ Emily said, giving her a quick hug.

‘Thanks,’ Sasha said. She couldn’t remember feeling happier than this.

Finn switched with Kyra, while Meili moved into the midfield, replacing Hani. Harper had the kick-off.

Brrrp!

Sasha loved watching her team play, and this was the Fever at their best. Harper passed to Meili, who dribbled down the sideline. Finn was there to take the pass. Sasha watched as he was brought up short by an Astonfield boy.

‘Wow!’ Sasha exclaimed as her best friend pulled off a perfect Maradona to dodge past and head for goal. He booted the ball to Sam, who passed to Charlie. The Astonfield goalkeeper deflected the ball.

‘Two minutes to go,’ Kyah called.

Sasha couldn't stand still as she watched the Fever and Astonfield tackle and dribble, neither side able to get a clear break.

'One minute,' Kyah called.

Meili stole the ball and charged back through the midfield. Sasha looked from Hani to Kyra, standing with her on the sideline. They grinned.

'Go Fever!' they yelled together.

Meili passed to Charlie, who kicked to Sam. Sasha saw Finn struggling to dodge his opponent, but then suddenly he was free. Sam saw it too. He faked, then cut across to the right, sending the ball to the top of the penalty box. Finn didn't hesitate. He kicked low and hard, sending the ball into the back right corner of the goal.

Brrrp!

'That's game,' Kyah called out.

The Fever shook hands with the Aston-field players and then crowded together, sharing hugs and high-fives. It had been a tough match against good-spirited opponents.

Emily and Lydia called them back. They had to clear the pitch because the Socceroos were about to come out for the second half of their match. As she headed towards the tunnel, Sasha glanced

up at the stands. She saw a little girl looking at her. Sasha waved. The girl looked so excited as she waved back, grabbing her dad's hand and pointing. As Sasha stepped into the darkness of the tunnel she made herself a promise. She would work hard and one day she'd be back at Accor Stadium wearing the Matildas green-and-gold.

*

The Socceroos friendly was a thriller. The USA came out firing after the half-time break, quickly levelling at one-all. But the Socceroos didn't give up. The Fever screamed themselves hoarse, encouraging their heroes. Sasha couldn't stop laughing as Crabbie did his own version of Andrew Redmayne's goal dance as the Socceroos goalie saved multiple USA attempts. Then

Ajdin Hrustic was awarded a penalty. Despite the distance, he went for goal, firing the ball over the heads of his opponents and into the net with pinpoint precision.

Full-time. The Socceroos had won 2–1.

Sasha watched her teammates as they moved around, mingling with their families. She couldn't believe it was over already. Finn was hugging his mum tightly. Sasha had never seen his smile so big.

'Hey,' she said as both her dads wrapped her up in a hug.

'We're so proud of you,' Paps said.

'Thanks,' she said. This was the best night of her life.

Way too soon it was time to go, but first Coach called them all together.

'I'm so proud of you all.' She smiled. 'I know it's been a big night, but I have one more piece of exciting news before you go.'

Sasha glanced at Kyra, raising her eyebrows. Kyra just shrugged.

'You've been invited to this year's High Potential Pathway Program,' Coach said.

Sasha was confused. She knew how tough it was to get into that program. It was for the best of the best. Australia's future stars.

'Who has, Coach?' Sasha asked quietly. 'Who's been invited?'

Coach was beaming. 'All of you.'

Everyone started talking at once, but Sasha stood quietly, taking it in. The Fever had played at Accor Stadium and now they had the chance to train with the best coaches and young players in Australia. She had no idea what the future held, but she knew she was happy to be sharing it with the Merridale Fever. Her team. Her football family.

THE MERRIDALE FEVER

Kyra Williams

Sam Elrick

Sasha Parry

Finn Sadler

Charles 'Crabbie' Cannon

Katarina 'Kat' Horvat

Harper Brown

Hani Hasan

Meili Chen

Luka Horvat

Ava Trent

Charlie Robertson

ABOUT THE AUTHOR

Kristin Darell has been a passionate storyteller since she was a child. Whether it was making up adventures with her twin sister, or writing about the world around her, she was rarely found without a pen and paper in hand. As an adult, she made this passion her life. She worked as a broadcast news and sports journalist for major Australian news organisations for more than twenty years.

After the birth of her two children, Kristin re-focused her attention on writing for children. As an author, she has contributed to children's writing anthologies. Football Fever is her debut junior fiction series.

Kristin is a strong advocate for children's literature, working as the Program Manager for the Australian Children's Laureate Foundation. She lives on Sydney's northern beaches with her husband, two children, two dogs, pet snake and three-legged pygmy bearded dragon.